To Luis, Patrice, and Nelson Poveda
To Gaspard and Rémi
—Élise Fontenaille

To David and Mo, with thanks,
and to my grandparents, whom I never met
—Violeta Lópiz

At the Drop of a Cat

Written by Élise Fontenaille
Illustrated by Violeta Lópiz

Translated from French by
Karin Snelson & Emilie Robert Wong

Enchanted Lion Books
NEW YORK

I turned six this year, and I'm learning to read and write.
I really like it. I practice at Luis's house. He's my grandpa.
He takes care of me a lot. Every Wednesday, and on Sundays, too.
He lives in a little house he built himself, surrounded by a garden bursting with incredible fruits and vegetables.
The garden feels like a whole other world.
Whenever it's nice outside, I sit out there at a little wooden table with my pencils and notebooks.

My mom says Luis has a green thumb.
The minute he plants a seed in the ground, it sprouts right up.
His green beans climb all the way to the sky, his artichokes grow as big as heads, and his leeks line up like a row of soldiers.
"I've never seen anything like it," says Mom.
All the other gardeners are jealous of Luis and his garden.
Luis likes to say: "The earth is my mother."

Luis speaks bird language.

When he talks to the chickadees, they talk back.
He knows all the garden birds by name.
He's taught me: oriole, chickadee, robin, sparrow, nightingale, starling...

Luis talks with his cat, too. Her name is Diabola.
They don't always agree.

Luis isn't from here.

He has an accent because he's from Spain.
He walked here all by himself when he was eleven years old.
He crossed mountains and hills and the countryside until
he got to France. He was running away from a terrible war.

Dad told me Luis didn't have a chance to be a kid.

He never went to school.

When he was my age, he was already working hard in the fields.
He never learned how to read or write, not even his name.
There aren't any books or newspapers anywhere in his house.
The walls are covered with pictures of flowers and animals
he drew himself.

Sometimes, we draw together in the garden.
His drawings are always better than mine.
Dad says Luis is as good as Henri Rousseau,
and he is a really famous painter.

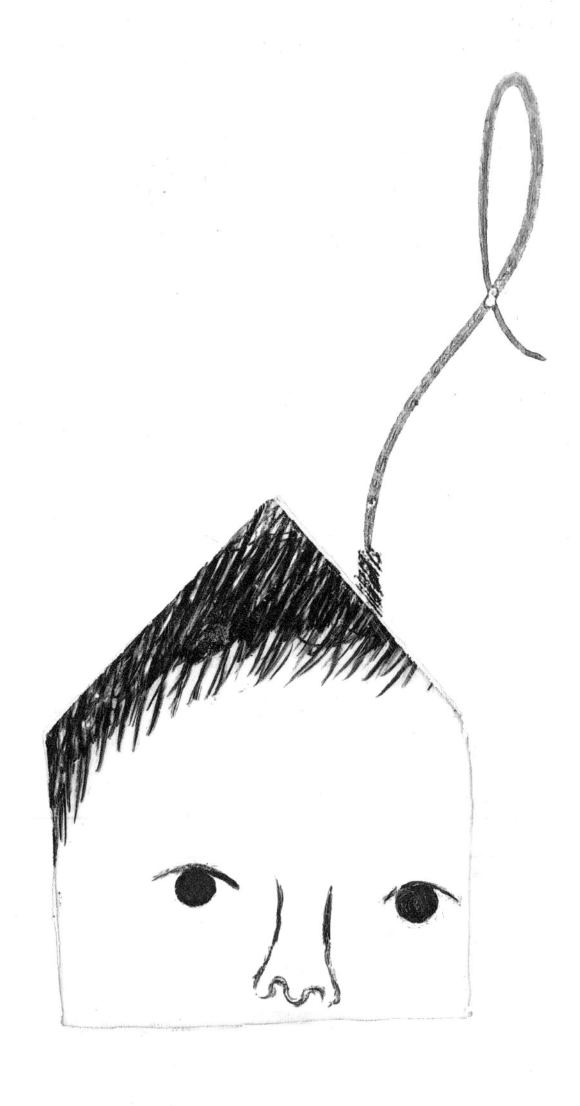

The other day, I got out my notebook and started writing.
Luis leaned over my shoulder, watching me draw my letters.
"Want me to teach you?" I asked him.
"Oh, it's a little late for me to learn now," he sighed.
"My head is tired."

I love the way Luis talks.
He's always saying:
"At the drop of a cat."
And now I say it all the time, too.
It means right away, without delay!

The other day at school, my teacher corrected me.
"We say: At the drop of a *hat!*"
I wanted to explain why I liked cat better,
but I didn't end up saying anything.

Luis spent a lot of time working on construction sites
when he was young. He didn't have a house,
so he slept in camper trailers.
I think I'd like living in a camper trailer...
I'd feel like I was always on vacation.

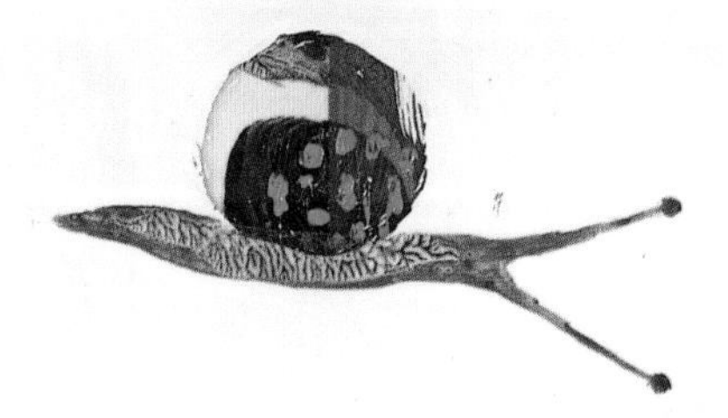

Another thing about Luis is that he is *such* a great cook. There's always something baking or simmering, so his house smells good.

He says I am "the apple of his pie," which means he really likes me. Or I am "the apple of his *eye!*" if you are my teacher.

We like to go to the meadow together to pick wild plants. Some are safe to eat, but be careful! Some are poisonous. You can't learn how to tell the difference from a book, so Luis shows me.

"A wild carrot smells good, like a carrot should. Hemlock looks like a carrot, too, but smells like a stinky dead mouse. If a cow eats even a little bit, it won't live through the night."

My grandpa has tattoos all over his arms: a rose, a knife,
a mermaid, a boat... memories from when he was young.
I daydream about his tattoos, and draw them in my notebook.
One day Luis said, "Back then, no one messed with me.
When I was twenty, fighting didn't scare me..."
He was digging with a spade and wearing an undershirt,
the sleeveless kind he calls "my marcel."
I told him, "I'd really like a marcel, too."
The very next Sunday, he found one for me at the market.
As soon as I put it on, I looked like a tough guy.

Whenever it's nice outside, Luis sings and plays his guitar under the cherry tree. The birds sing back to him. Diabola rubs her head against his hand while he strums the strings. It makes me laugh. She's always doing that. It doesn't bother Luis at all, he loves cats.
I sing with him in Spanish, even though I don't understand all of it. It's a song about women, hearts, and butterflies. *Corazón, mariposa*... I like these words a lot.

One day at the end of the school year,
I read a poem out loud to him, two whole pages:
"The Cat and the Bird" by Jacques Prévert.
It was June, and the cherry tree was loaded
with black cherries. The birds wouldn't stop stealing
the fruit, and Diabola was dreaming of catching a bird.

"You did it! You can read and write," my grandpa said.
He got up and came back with an enormous package.
A guitar, just for me!
I tried it out—*dzing, dzing*.
I was on top of the world!
Luis showed me how to play a few chords.
"It's a little big for you now," he said.
"But don't worry, your fingers will grow."

www.enchantedlion.com

First English-language edition, published in 2023
by Enchanted Lion Books, 248 Creamer Street,
Studio 4, Brooklyn, NY 11231
First published in France as *Les poings sur les îles*

Book design by Eugenia Mello

A CIP is on record with the Library of Congress
ISBN 978-1-59270-382-1
Printed in China by RR Donnelley
Asia Printing Solutions Ltd.

First Printing